God Made KITTENS

by Marian Bennett   illustrated by Kathryn Hutton

Tenth Printing, 1992

When God made kittens,
  He must have laughed
    to see them play and run.

He made them to pounce,

jump, and roll,

and have all kinds of fun!

God made kittens
  with warm, soft fur,

with bright, shining eyes,
and a deep purr.

Kittens like to play
hide and seek,

follow the leader,

and chase the ball.

They like to climb
on low tables,

and cabinets so tall.

Kittens have sharp teeth,
and tongues that feel like sand.

When a kitten licks you,
it tickles your hand.

Kittens come in many colors—
brown, black, and white.

Some are all colors.
They're quite a sight!

Kittens' tails may be large,
or they may be small.

But God made the Manx cat
to have no tail at all.

A kitten is curious about
small things and places.

He sometimes goes
where he shouldn't be—

in a tiny box,
behind a book,

and sometimes
up in a tree.

Kittens like warm milk,
and soft beds,

someone to pet them,
and scratch their heads.

God made kittens
   as cute as can be,

to bring happiness and love—

to you and to me!

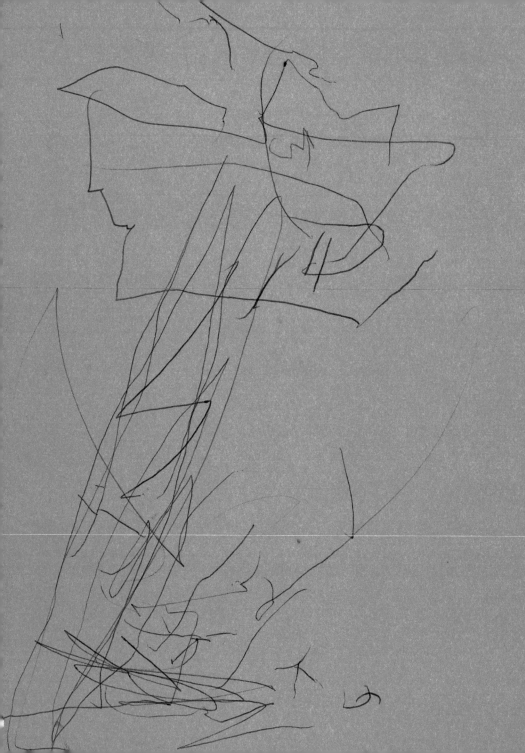